THE
AUTHOR VISIT
FROM THE
BLACK LAGOON®

Get more monster-sized laughs from

The Black Lagoon®

THE
AUTHOR VISIT
FROM THE
BLACK LAGOON®

NEVER SEEN WITHOUT HIS HAT ON

NEW BOOK IDEAS

MIKE THALER

LUNCH

ALWAYS DRESSES IN YELLOW

NEVER WEARS A WATCH

by Mike Thaler
Illustrated by Jared Lee

SCHOLASTIC INC.

New York Toronto London Auckland
Sydney Mexico City New Delhi Hong Kong

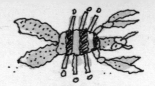

To authors of all ages
—M.T.

To Mike Thaler,
my favorite author
—J.L.

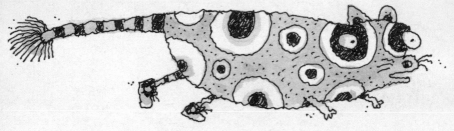

ISBN 978-0-545-27327-5

Text copyright © 2010 by Mike Thaler
Illustrations copyright © 2010 by Jared D. Lee Studio, Inc.

All rights reserved. Published by Scholastic Inc.

SCHOLASTIC, LITTLE APPLE, and associated logos are trademarks and/or
registered trademarks of Scholastic Inc. BLACK LAGOON is a registered
trademark of Mike Thaler and Jared D. Lee Studio, Inc. All rights reserved.
Lexile is a registered trademark of MetaMetrics, Inc.

18 17 16 15   20 21/0

Printed in the U.S.A.   40
First printing, November 2010

CONTENTS

CHAPTER 1
BOOKING AN AUTHOR

MRS. GREEN →

ISN'T THIS EXCITING, CLASS?

A real live author is going to come to our school. I guess that's better than having a real dead one. There are so many to choose from. There are tons of good books.

NOTE: A **TON** IS 2000 POUNDS

Mrs. Green says that if all the good books were put end to end, you could read all the way to the moon and back. You'd really be spaced-out.

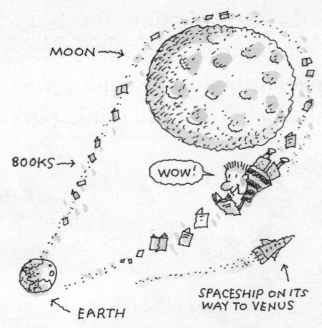

MOON →

BOOKS →

WOW!

EARTH

SPACESHIP ON ITS WAY TO VENUS

Eric says that if you put all the authors end to end they'd look pretty silly

YOU CAN NEVER USE ENOUGH GARLIC.

I'm on the author selection committee with Eric, Derek, Penny, Randy, Freddy, and Doris. Freddy wants to invite a cookbook author. Penny and Doris are pushing for a girls' book author. "*Cute* little kittens, *sweet* little horsies, and *princess* ballerinas" . . . pink, pink, pink.

THE AUTHOR SELECTION COMMITTEE

HUBIE

ERIC

DEREK

PENNY

RANDY

DORIS

FREDDY

TAILSPIN

HAS NO AUTHORITY WHATSOEVER

Eric, Derek, and I are holding out for a monster book author like Gravely Stone, Reggy Mortis, or Dinah Sore.

DO MONSTERS GO TO THE DENTIST?

BY GRAVELY STONE

INCREDIBLE →

NIGHT NUISANCE

HILARIOUS! ↑

VOTED MOST CREATIVE →

MY LIFE AS A RABBIT VAMPIRE

BY REGGY MORTIS

11

Randy says authors with two initials in their names are better writers than ones without any.

"Like who?" asks Eric.

"J.K. Rowling, E. B. White, and C. S. Lewis," answers Randy.

"That's silly," says Penny. "There are great writers with no initials."

J.K. ROWLING   E. B. WHITE   C. S. LEWIS

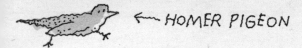

"Like who?" snickers Randy.

"Like Shakespeare, Tolstoy, and Homer," says Penny.

"There's even a great writer with no name," I say.

"Who?" says everybody.

"Annie Nonymous." I smile.

SHAKESPEARE   TOLSTOY   HOMER

Our librarian, Mrs. Beamster, would like Mr. Webster, the guy who wrote the dictionary. And Mrs. Green wants a Blueberry Award winner.

HERE'S A PICTURE OF HIM.

TINY BIRD (EXACT SIZE) →

We can't please everybody, so we finally decide on Penny Inkblot. I've never read any of her books, but now I'll have to. In fact, everyone in school will, too.

15

CHAPTER 2
CHECKING THEM OUT

AUTHOR→

HELLO.

←ARTHUR

We ask Mrs. Beamster about writers.

She smiles.

"There are lots of good writers. They stretch like a mountain range throughout history. Some of the peaks are William Shake-A-Spear, who wrote plays, Charles Dickens, who wrote novels, and William Butler Yeats, who wrote poetry."

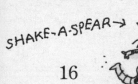

SHAKE-A-SPEAR→

BUTLER→

"Are any of them alive?" I ask.

"They're all alive when you open the pages of their books," answers Mrs. Beamster.

"Do they do school visits?" I ask.

"Not anymore," says Mrs. Beamster.

←PENNY   ←DIME

"Have you ever heard of Penny Inkblot?" asks Penny.

"She's a terrific writer," answers Mrs. Beamster.

"Do you have any of her books?" I ask.

"Lots, but they're all checked out."

"Bummer!" But it's not too bad because now Mom will take me to the bookstore tonight.

HUBIE, WAIT UP!

← ERIC

NEIGHBOR'S ANNOYING DOG

CHAPTER 3
DESTINATION IMAGINATION

After school, Eric and I have a deep conversation.

"I'd like to be an author when I grow up," I say.

"I'd like to be an astronaut," says Eric.

"Why?" I ask.

THIS IS SANTA, NOT AN AUTHOR →

"When you're an astronaut, you get to travel to other worlds. Why do you want to be a writer?"

"When you're a writer, you get to create other worlds."

"For instance?" asks Eric.

"For instance, Middle-earth, Wonderland, Oz, and Hogwarts." I answer.

"You mean those places *aren't* real?"

FOR THERE WAS A PLACE LIKE NO OTHER WHERE THE SKY WAS GREEN AND THE GRASS WAS BLUE...

WRITER AT WORK →

RING! RING! RING

TAP! TAP! TAP!

"They're all real in our imaginations."

"How about Treasure Island?"

"Imagination," I smile.

"You mean I can't fly there on vacation?"

"Sure you can . . . in a book."

HUBIE, THERE'S THE PIRATE SHIP!

CARNIVAL BARKER ⟶

COME ONE. COME ALL.

CHAPTER 4
I LOVE A PARADE

TAKE ME HOME.

After dinner, Mom takes me to the bookstore. I love to browse. I walk up and down the aisles. Every book is waiting to tell me something. The covers are like carnival barkers shouting, "Open me, read me, and I'll tell you wonderful things. I'll make you laugh, I'll make you cry, I can even make you fly."

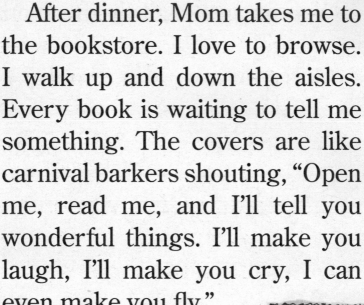

MOM, WHY IS THE BOOKSTORE ALWAYS BUSY?

BECAUSE PEOPLE LOVE BOOKS.

BOOKSTORE

MORE PARKING ACROSS THE STREET

25

I finally make it to Penny Inkblot's books. All her titles sound cool: *The Underwear-wolf, Drac-cola, Dinosaurs in Space, You Can't Chew Gum with Your Nose, Fangenstein,* and *Zitwit.*

IT'S GOING TO BE HARD TO CHOOSE ONE.

It takes me until closing to choose. But as they're shutting out the lights, I pick *Drac-cola*. I can't wait to read it.

HOW YOU CAN SPOT AN AUTHOR

READS HIS BOOKS TO ANYONE WILLING TO LISTEN

PEN READY TO SIGN BOOKS FOR AUTOGRAPH SEEKERS

CARRIES A SHOULDER BAG FULL OF PENCILS, PAPER, AND NOTES

HAS WEAK LEGS FROM SITTING FOR HOURS AT HIS WRITING DESK

CAN BE FOUND NEAR HIS BOOKS AT LIBRARIES AND BOOKSTORES

29

CHAPTER 5
READY TO READ

I start reading in the van, even though I get a little dizzy. The book is about a vampire that drinks soda pop instead of blood. A vampire that drives a van would be called a *vanpire*. He breaks his fangs off biting into a cola can. All the other vampires make fun of him. They call him "deadhead" and "toothless ruthless." It's a biting satire.

← FANG MARKS

SODA

He reads about a new-fangled invention that might help, so his mom takes him to the dentist to get a set of false fangs. This is really a story you can sink your teeth into.

SON, OPEN YOUR MOUTH WIDER.

FANG ↓

33

That night I have a dream. . . . I'm a famous author. My book has won the Blueberry Award and I've been invited to Transylvania to talk at a night school. I go in and all the kids are vampires. It's a holiday—*Fangsgiving*. I'm there for the whole vampire week: *Moanday*, *Toothday*, *Veinsday*, *Thirstday*, and *Frightday*.

35

My teeth start getting longer and longer till they touch my toes. I'm going batty. When I give my speech at the assembly, all the kids are coffin and flyin' around the auditorium. No one's read my books and they're all disappointed because they had asked for a dead author.

I wake up in a sweat and go and check my teeth. They're just regular size. "Phew!"

WHAT'S HAPPENING?

TEETH

CHAPTER 6
FOOTNOTES

In the morning on the school bus, everyone's talking about the author visit. Eric says not to sit in the first three rows unless you have a raincoat or an umbrella. He says some authors spit when they speak. Derek says they love to talk about themselves.

HA, HA, HA.

"This is my dog. This is my cat. This is my coat. This is my hat."

And they bring pictures of everything they own. Randy says they write children's books because they don't know many words.

HOW BIG IS YOUR VOCABULARY?

READ US A STORY.

DAISY IS THREE.

LITTLE MONSTERS.

39

Penny says they've never really grown up themselves and are just big kids. Doris says they're all rich and ride in limousines and live in mansions. Freddy heard they get a royalty, so they're all kings and queens and they rule the nation of imagination.

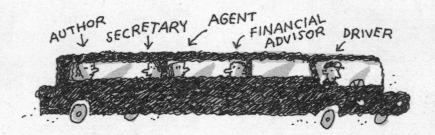

AUTHOR   SECRETARY   AGENT   FINANCIAL ADVISOR   DRIVER

Penny says that's silly—that they're regular people just like us and we could be writers if we worked hard enough. I agree with Penny about that.

← CROWN

WHAT IS A GHOST WRITER?

TAP! TAP! TAP!

(A) THEY ONLY WRITE ON HALLOWEEN.

(B) THEY CREATE NEW GHOST TALES.

(C) THEY WRITE THE BOOK AND SOMEONE ELSE RECEIVES THE CREDIT.

(D) IT'S A DEAD AUTHOR WHO COMES BACK TO LIFE TO WRITE MORE BOOKS.

ANSWER ON PAGE 44.

CHAPTER 7
GETTING READY

HOUSTON, WE HAVE A PROBLEM.

After we've read all of Penny Inkblot's books, we discuss them.

I liked *Dinosaurs in Space* the best. It was about a prehistoric future. It gave me a lot to think about. What if prehistoric times haven't happened yet? Or what if we find dinosaurs on other planets?

COMET →

↑ COMET

Derek liked *The Underwear-wolf*. He said it's about a kid whose underwear gets hairy every full moon.

Freddy chose *You Can't Chew Gum with Your Nose*. He said he tried it and had to go to the emergency room.

SORRY WE'RE LATE. WE JUST CAME FROM A TEN-CAR PILEUP.

WHAT'S WRONG WITH YOUR SON?

HE HAS GUM STUCK UP HIS NOSE.

COME IN NUMBER 7, WE HAVE A PYTHON BITE ON ELM STREET.

Eric liked *Fangenstein*, cause you get two monsters for the price of one.

Penny picked *Zitwit*. It's a story about a very smart pimple that goes to college. It does very well, grows popular, and gets a swelled head when it's picked to be class president.

Next we all write our own stories and make our own book covers.

Penny was right—we're *all* authors.

CONGRATULATIONS. YOU GOT A B-PUS ON THE EXAM.

B+

←—TEACHER

PIMPLE→

I BROUGHT THE WELCOME WAGON.

CHAPTER 8
GREETINGS

The welcome banner is up, and tomorrow our author is coming.

Penny and I are picked to greet her and be her guides. I was picked because I read the most books for read-a-thon, and Penny was picked because her name is Penny.

WELCOME PENNY INKBLOT

WILL BE CARRIED LIVE ON ALL THE CABLE STATIONS

JET

SCHOOL

BUSH

BASKETBALL

We get to stay with the author all day. Even have lunch with her! I'm really excited. I can hardly wait to meet Penny Inkblot.

BIRDMAN →

CHAPTER 9
BAD PRESS

That night I have another dream. Penny and I are standing in front of the school when a shadow covers the yard. A limousine as long as a train rolls up and stops. Penny Inkblot steps out. She's wearing a crown, a fur coat, and diamonds on every finger.

49

We say hello and start to give our welcome poem, but she walks right by us and into the school. In the auditorium when I try to introduce her, she grabs the mike and starts to tell us all about herself.

She has pictures of her chair, her desk, and her mansion. Then she reads us all her newest masterpiece—*The Phone Book*. There are no pictures!

FIRST OF ALL, I'D LIKE TO SAY HOW FORTUNATE YOU ARE FOR ME TO BE HERE TODAY.

PEN
INK

She says she doesn't sign books, but she has a rubber stamp and stamps our foreheads as we leave. I wake up bumping my head on the bedpost.

SPEED IT UP. I HAVE TO FLY TO PARIS FOR ANOTHER AWARDS BANQUET.

52

Today's the day I was looking forward to. But now I'm not so sure.

CHAPTER 10
JUST RIGHT

Penny and I are standing in front of our school. It's great to be out of class.

We're watching the free world go by when a small car drives up. An old one at that. It parks and out steps a nice lady in a suit. I guess she left her crown at home.

She smiles and says, "Hello."

We answer, "We're Penny and Hubie, and we're the two who have been picked to welcome you."

She shakes our hands as we continue, "We've read all your books and will write a long letter telling you how to make them all better."

"Well, thank you, Penny and Hubie." She shakes our hands again.

> IT'S NICE MEETING YOU.

> HOW ABOUT ME?

"We're here to show you the way, and we hope you have a very good day."

"Thank you."

"So just follow us into the school cause we think that you are really cool."

YOU HAVE A BEAUTIFUL SCHOOL.

THEY MOWED THE GRASS YESTERDAY.

THANK YOU. OUR PRINCIPAL OWNS IT.

"Well, thank you. I also think you're cool."

"My name's Penny, too," says Penny.

"How nice," says Penny Inkblot.

57

CHAPTER 11
STRAIGHT FROM THE AUTHOR'S MOUTH

Well, to make a short story long, Penny, as she told us to call her, really was cool. She loves to write and feels very lucky to be an author. She said that we could be authors, too, and she told

BASIC TOOLS TO BE AN AUTHOR

AND AN IDEA!

← COMFORTABLE CHAIR

PAPER ↓

← LAMP

PENCILS →

TABLE ↑

WASTEBASKET ↑

Mrs. Beamster to put our books in the library next to hers. She said all you need to be a writer is a pencil, a piece of paper, and your imagination. She said our imaginations are as good as hers but you have to exercise them every day, just like a muscle.

She says she is working on a new book—*Lip Bowling*.

Sounds like a winner.

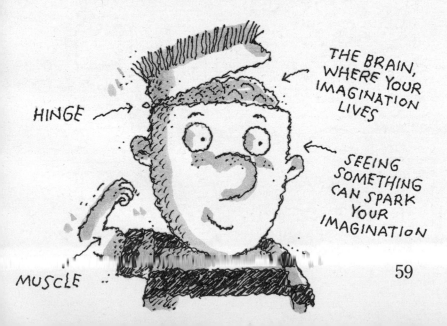

HINGE →

THE BRAIN, WHERE YOUR IMAGINATION LIVES

SEEING SOMETHING CAN SPARK YOUR IMAGINATION

MUSCLE

59

Then she gave us lots of tips about writing, like have a good title. Sometimes a whole story can grow out of a title, or out of a good first line. For instance, "I woke up this morning and my bed was on the ceiling."

12 THINGS YOU CAN ASK AN AUTHOR

1. HOW MANY BOOKS HAVE YOU WRITTEN?

2. DID YOU GO TO COLLEGE OR A WRITING SCHOOL?

3. DO YOU HAVE A REAL JOB?

4. HOW LONG DOES IT TAKE YOU TO WRITE A BOOK?

5. DO YOU OWN YOUR OWN JET?

6. HOW OLD WERE YOU WHEN YOU WROTE YOUR FIRST BOOK?

7. DO YOU WRITE EVERY DAY?

8. WHERE DO YOU GET YOUR IDEAS FOR A NEW BOOK?

9. DO YOU USE A COMPUTER OR NOTEPAD WHEN YOU WRITE?

10. DO YOU LIVE ON YOUR OWN ISLAND?

11. DO YOU DRAW THE PICTURES?

12. DO YOU KNOW ANY MOVIE STARS?

She said we can be anything we dream, if we're willing to work hard enough. She said we should start today, and if we want to be writers, we should write something every day.

So when I got home from school, instead of turning on the TV, I wrote a story that started, "When I went to sleep, my bed was on the ceiling." It's called Upside-down Dreams.

I dedicated it to my friend Penny Inkblot, and tomorrow I'm going to ask Mrs. Beamster to put it in the school library.

Then I'll be an author, too.